THIS IS ME!

RHYMES OF CHILDHOOD

Edited By Roseanna Caswell

First published in Great Britain in 2023 by:

YoungWriters®
— Est. 1991 —

Young Writers
Remus House
Coltsfoot Drive
Peterborough
PE2 9BF
Telephone: 01733 890066
Website: www.youngwriters.co.uk

Printed and bound in the UK by BookPrintingUK
Website: www.bookprintinguk.com
YB0572H

FOREWORD

For Young Writers' latest competition This Is Me,
we asked primary school pupils to look inside
themselves, to think about what makes them unique,
and then write a poem about it! They rose to the
challenge magnificently and the result is this fantastic
collection of poems in a variety of poetic styles.

Here at Young Writers our aim is to encourage creativity
in children and to inspire a love of the written word, so
it's great to get such an amazing response, with some
absolutely fantastic poems. It's important for children to
focus on and celebrate themselves and this competition
allowed them to write freely and honestly, celebrating
what makes them great, expressing their hopes and
fears, or simply writing about their favourite things.
This Is Me gave them the power of words. The result
is a collection of inspirational and moving poems that
also showcase their creativity and writing ability.

I'd like to congratulate all the young poets
in this anthology, I hope this inspires them
to continue with their creative writing.

CONTENTS

Ladeside Primary School, Larbert

Lucy Sellwood (10)	55
Erin Smith (9)	56
Mya Snedden (11)	57
Alyssa Stirling (11)	58
Mason Douglas (11)	59
Libby Smith (8)	60
Tyler McDonald (11)	61
Isabella Kanzidis (13)	62
Daisy Chipulu (9)	63
Sonny Gillie (11)	64
Calin Cassidy (10)	65
Olivia Bain (10)	66

Milesmark Primary School, Rumblingwell

Ruaridh Rees (10)	67
Ellie Fiona Cramb (10)	68
Munroe Candlish (10)	70
Ilyas Razzaq (11)	71
Maia Harker (10)	72
Kerr Kelso (10)	73
Rylie Smart (10)	74
Theerathan Halliday (11)	75
Lucie Morrison (11)	76
Connor Henderson (10)	77
Ben Fraser (10)	78
Lailah Symon-Edwards (11)	79
Abigail Morton (10)	80

Old Monkland Primary And Nursery School, Coatbridge

Lilien Somogyi (9)	81
Freya Kay (9)	82
James Roy (9)	83
Mollie Brankin (9)	84
Amber Honeyman (8)	85
Logan Cossutta (7)	86
Rubie-Rose Downes (8)	87
Oscar Brodie (9)	88
Arabella Lyall (8)	89

Korey Love (8)	90
Freya Sanderson (8)	91
Lilly Gardiner (9)	92
Cody Hillan (8)	93
Lewis Calder (8)	94
Lorena Small (9)	95
Josh Lawrie (8)	96

RGS Dodderhill School, Droitwich Spa

Cecily Smith (7)	97
Violet Craze (9)	98
Olivia Lloyd-Allum (10)	100
Lucy Wainwright (9)	102
Lola Herriotts (8)	104
Alby White (8)	105
Eloise Hogwood (9)	106
Isabella Chance (9)	108
Isabella Gough (9)	109
Grace Hogwood (9)	110
Lorianna Mason (9)	111
Joseph Spencer (10)	112
Madeleine Sisson (8)	113
Lily Spencer (7)	114
James Spencer (10)	115
Cameron Hollingworth (7)	116
Edie Banyard (7)	117

St Mary's Catholic Voluntary Academy, Marple Bridge

Annelle Campbell (8)	118
Iris Mulryan (9)	120
Rain Claridge (8)	122
Callum Deegan (9)	124
Margot Emery (7)	126
Herbie Keene (10)	127
Lucia Tognarelli (8)	128
Inès Vibert	129
Kitty Groarke-Booth (7)	130
Jacob Jensen (11)	131
Leo Brown (7)	132
Isaac Jones (9)	133

Jonah Young (10)	134	Finley Wass (7)	177
Anya Butler (10)	135	Maria Wall (6)	178
Lucia Gianferrari (8)	136	Matilda Stanley (7)	179
Isaac Chrippes (10)	137	Jack Brislane (7)	180
James Tolley (7)	138	Isabelle Payne (11)	181
Florence Royle (7)	139	Sophie Bradbury (6)	182
Amelia Smith (7)	140	Evie Russell (6)	183
Harry Woodhead (8)	141	Oliver Moores (6)	184
Jack Callaghan (6)	142	Anna Webb (10)	185
Lydia Crosthwaite (7)	143	Gracie Heaps (10)	186
Judy Mylrea (10)	144	Daisy Robinson-Bocking (6)	187
Orry Mylrea (10)	145	Jacob Russell (8)	188
Florence Harrison (8)	146	Jemima M	189
Lois Tomlinson (8)	147	Maddie Percy (8)	190
Austin Gallogly-Frame (6)	148	Isaiah G (9)	191
Annie-Mae Field (7)	149	Freddie Muncaster (6)	192
Pauric Beetham (6)	150	George Bullock	193
Niamh Barlow (7)	151	Charles Whitehead (6)	194
Aoife Wood	152	Noah Bullock (8)	195
George Percy (6)	153	Diana Akhondzadeh (7)	196
Ella Crosthwaite (10)	154	Finnley Chrippes (6)	197
Jonah Wood (6)	155	Joshua Rose (7)	198
Annie Thompson (6)	156	Jacob Anthony Derwent	199
Joe Buckley (10)	157	Chapman (6)	
Maria Hockey (7)	158	Caleb Rose (10)	200
Daniel Lee (7)	159	Nico Wilmott-Jones (7)	201
Nicco Tognarelli (6)	160	Isaac Payne (8)	202
Lottie Mayers (6)	161	George Oates (10)	203
George Drake (7)	162	Quinn Hall (8)	204
William Mayers (8)	163	Bella Clark (7)	205
Mathieu Vibert (7)	164	Aine Deegan (6)	206
Annabelle Tsopanou (7)	165	Caleb Smiley (8)	207
Olivia Smiley	166	Tadhg Curley (7)	208
Grace Walker (7)	167	Isla Harrison (7)	209
Daniel Purrier (6)	168	George Muncaster (6)	210
Tom Wiedemann (10)	169	Jack Challinor (8)	211
Evan Freeman (8)	170	Teddy Carter (6)	212
James Camm (6)	171		
Lucy Carter (9)	172		
Harry Wiedemann (7)	173		
Caitlin Camm (8)	174		
Lily Sharrocks (8)	175		
Sofia Evans	176		

THE POEMS

THE POEMS

Zombs Royale

Z ombie mode is not fun

O verpowered describes the XM8

M y favourite gun is the AWP rifle

B est mode is the mystery mode

S uperpowers have too many sweats

R everse impulses are fun

O p is how you pronounce AWP

Y oshiClapz is a Zombs Royale YouTuber

A ppleman is a skin

L evelling up the battle pass is easy

E xtremely hard to win.

Jeronimo Lynch (9)

Alexander Peden Primary School And Nursery, Harthill

This Is Me

T urtles are my favourite animal
H ats are my favourite accessory
I am a boy
S teak pie is a great pie

I love playing football
S marties are my favourite sweets

M y life is great
E verybody likes me.

Jack Dickson (9)

Alexander Peden Primary School And Nursery, Harthill

The Lovely Earth And God Who Made It

I love the Earth, it is our planet
I am very energetic right now and feel very weird
I want to game on Roblox because I am fun to
play with
I want to go to Ibrox to watch the phenomenal
football
Because Messi is the GOAT
This is me
Thank you, Earth.

Paisley Stevenson (9)
Alexander Peden Primary School And Nursery, Harthill

A Sprinkle Of That

To make me, you will need:
A pinch of mischief
A handful of loud
A little scoop of rude
A bowl full of loving
A cup full of singing, maybe even dancing
A sprinkle of bad
A bucketful of good
And finally...
A spoonful of cheeky.

Lucy Marshall (10)

Alexander Peden Primary School And Nursery, Harthill

Everything To Make Me

To create me, you will need:
A little bit of nice but a big cup of kind
Half a cup of caring and a full cup of reading
But give me two full cups of my favourite dancing
These are the things that make me, me.

Freya McKee (9)
Alexander Peden Primary School And Nursery, Harthill

This Is Me

A kennings poem

I am a...
Good drawer
Early riser
Light sleeper
Sweet eater
Gymnastics lover
Art lover
White tiger lover
Roblox lover
Video game lover
And finally...
Caring person.

Laci Worral (10)

Alexander Peden Primary School And Nursery, Harthill

Fortnite Battle Pass

F irst place

O nly up Fortnite

R are weapons

T ry hard

N o cheating

I am a pro at Fortnite

T ry not to rage

E xcellent at Fortnite.

Ollie McKillop (10)

Alexander Peden Primary School And Nursery, Harthill

Me

A kennings poem

I am a...
Good gamer
Funny person
Tony Hawk pro skater
Great skateboarder
Queen fan
Rock music fan
Outside lover
Boy with ADHD
I am Kyle.

Kyle Cefferty (10)
Alexander Peden Primary School And Nursery, Harthill

Me

A kennings poem

I am a...
Footballer
Man United fanboy
Rangers fanboy
Gamer
Guitarist
Musician
Laptop lover
And finally...
My name is Cole.

Cole Brown (10)

Alexander Peden Primary School And Nursery, Harthill

Recipe For A Poppy

To make me, you will need:
Many dashes of summer sun
A squidge of snuggly nights with my mum
A sprinkle of excitement, a new day has begun
A spot of days out skipping, singing and love
50g of adventures beginning at sunrise and
returning at sunset
And a drop of relaxation in my head

Now you need to:
Add the dashes of summer sun
But also snowy, snuggly nights with my mum
Mix carefully. Don't let the ingredients fly up
in the air
As you slowly pour 50g of adventures in, my
energy builds up
Mix until a creamy texture
My squidge of excitement builds up inside
Then pour in my love and bake for ten minutes
until warm and loveable.

Poppy Jenner (9)
Clent Parochial Primary School, Holy Cross

Football, Football, Football

Racing up and down the pitch
Dribbling around cones with ease
Passing drills as sharp as quills
The beautiful game has begun

In the middle, it's where the playmaker lives
Then there's the left and right, a gruesome fright
The striker runs and scores again
The beautiful game has begun

At the back, they're a very fearsome group
In the goal, he's ready to pounce
They'll run around and never sit down
The beautiful game has begun

Back at my house, I'm off the TV
I'm in the garden, smiling with glee
Playing with friends from dawn til dusk
The beautiful game has begun.

Harry Isherwood (9)
Clent Parochial Primary School, Holy Cross

This Is Me!

I am kind and loving
Sweet and charming
Friendly and gentle to all the world
I love to swim and sing
I would think I'm almost perfect
I feel like a seal when I'm in seawater
And my singing is like a professional
I make friends in a second
They say they could laugh every day
I guess that means I'm funny
And I agree with them
But my teachers think the opposite
Calm, yet tender-hearted
Everybody calls me small
Size does not matter to me
But maybe a few inches would do
This is me!

Grace Robinson (9)

Clent Parochial Primary School, Holy Cross

Too Many Emotions

Too many emotions at once can make
Your head is a jumble or even mumbles
Sadness is making me feel badness
Straight over to anxiety is so boring

Happiness calls my name
But wait, what's blocking me...
Confusion is like a fusion of my brain lids dying

Over to you hyper
Woohoo! I'm excited now
But wait, not done yet

Anger, argh!
Why are you making me mad?
Got to get peace now
I'm calm
Wait, am I there?
Finally!
That's too many emotions!

Josh Horan (10)
Clent Parochial Primary School, Holy Cross

Me And My Brothers

I am me
I have two brothers, one is called Lee
My other brother is called Jamie
We have fun, even though
We always have to go
And even though
It was a long time ago
We all lived together
And we were happy, no matter the weather
But now, my brother, Lee
Has had a baby
And most times we miss each other
We will remember when we lived together
Helping one another
My brother, Jamie, has moved back in
Even though
It was a bit ago
We still love each other
Evenly so.

Grace Palmer-Duggan (10)

Clent Parochial Primary School, Holy Cross

Music Makes Us Feel

You press play on the music
Play whatever you want
You can have happy
You can have sad
You can have angry if you want
If you feel depressed
You might want a friend by your side
And you dance, you dance, you dance
Until you die
Music can make us feel the differences
Just like we have ours
But the thing is we're all a shining star
We have our moments
We have our times
But music makes us happy
Every single time.

Evie Worrod (10)
Clent Parochial Primary School, Holy Cross

This Is Me

Sometimes I'm happy
Sometimes I'm sad
Sometimes I'm joyful
And sometimes football mad

Animals I love
Animals I adore
Animals are brilliant
Aren't they super?

I want a lizard
A lizard is what I want
They can climb up trees
But heat is what they need

My life is incredible
My life is full of fun
This is me
This is my life
Thank you
And goodnight.

Harry Downing (9)
Clent Parochial Primary School, Holy Cross

Angry

My face goes red when I'm mad
I feel like I'm about to explode
I'm told to calm down
But nothing will ever work
I can't concentrate and I won't listen
I'll throw a tantrum and it will go on for about
five minutes
Then I'm put to ease and I calm down and stay still
Calm is what I'd like to be but I know I can't
because that's not me.

Sofia Long (9)
Clent Parochial Primary School, Holy Cross

What Am I?

I am fluffy and furry
With big brown eyes
I've got paws and a nose
And long flappy ears
What am I?

I like to run
And fetch balls
I drink water and eat food
I like to be stroked all the time
What am I?

I wag my tail when I'm happy
And sometimes I'm mischievous
Sometimes I'm sad, excited or glad
What am I?

Anna Clewlow (9)
Clent Parochial Primary School, Holy Cross

Singing!

Singing is like a gentle sound that can get you
to sleep
Singing is like a happy monster
Singing can be anything you want it to be
It can be a strong wind after a tragic fall of rain
It can be a tree dancing in the wind
It can be a chaotic party on a Friday night
It can be an angry monster flying in the sky
Singing is everything, it can be anything.

Layla Hartley (9)
Clent Parochial Primary School, Holy Cross

Football Is Life

I'm lightning in football boots
I'm the world's best defender
I'm a lion, strong and brave
I follow the rules
I often win my games
It's sometimes chucking it down
Or it's really hot
I'm like an eagle watching the ball
It's like a rocket when I shoot
My shot breaks the net
My football friends are like me.

Charles Richmond (9)
Clent Parochial Primary School, Holy Cross

Me With The Great Tiger

I read a book all about tigers
A great big tiger please beware
I wouldn't have known that it would be a wild tiger
Until it said something which made me wilder
For the notice that though it ate meat
It would have anyone else than me
In thinking this she was misled
But when I was done
Saying to myself, "I am really tired..."

Lyelah Penn (9)
Clent Parochial Primary School, Holy Cross

![YoungWriters Est. 1991]

My Mixed Emotions

Sometimes I'm sad
Sometimes I'm happy
Sometimes I'm joyful
Sometimes I'm silly
Sometimes I'm naughty
A bit of ADHD doesn't help me

I can be crazy
I can be mad
When I calm down, I can feel sad
When I play football, I start feeling glad

I'm happy being me and content I will be.

Harry Arthurs (10)
Clent Parochial Primary School, Holy Cross

This Is Me!

T en is my age for now

H obbies are gymnastics, netball and tennis

I love to learn new things

S ometimes I do a few cartwheels

I have one younger sibling

S ometimes we don't get along

M y favourite animal is a puppy

E lsie and Charlie are my friendly dogs.

Isabelle Craddock (10)

Clent Parochial Primary School, Holy Cross

My Imagination

Where will it take you?
Where will you go?
Art is imagination
How far will you go?

Soar through the sky
All the way to the moon

Maybe paint a friend
Or a dog
Let your imagination
Grow and grow

Where will it take you?
Where will you go?

Daisy Roberts (9)
Clent Parochial Primary School, Holy Cross

Anger!

I'll throw a tantrum, I'll slam my feet
I'll go so red and then I'll breathe
I'll punch, I'll kick and I will be so mean
I'll have a meltdown and then I'll scream
But I calm down and I have a smile
That lightens up the whole town
And this is me.

Millie Gilbert (10)
Clent Parochial Primary School, Holy Cross

Anger River

It can be deep
It can be shallow
It can be wide
It can be narrow
The smaller it is, I'm easier to break
The wider it is, I'm easier to take
Sometimes I'm sad
Sometimes I'm mad
But it gets better over time
I am myself and anger is mine.

Honey Roberts (11)
Clent Parochial Primary School, Holy Cross

The Shooting Star

A shooting star glides across the night
With a trail of silver, a tail of light
People wish upon them
People wish with hope
The wish will come true
Just wait and see
A shooting star represents me
As I shoot through the sky
With my trail of past behind me.

Tegan Gwynn (9)
Clent Parochial Primary School, Holy Cross

This Is Me!

T iny... a bit
H ave annoying habits
I love my family
S ometimes I cook with them

I like to play hide-and-seek
S ometimes I go shopping

M ainly use my iPad
E xcellent at English.

Eva Murdanaigum (10)
Clent Parochial Primary School, Holy Cross

Calm

Calm is where I feel my best
Calm is where I live
Calm is like the breeze above
Calm is the mountains I love
Calm is like flowers
Calm is like the sea
Calm is like nature
Calm is everything I see
And tranquillity is for me!

Harlow Deakin (9)

Clent Parochial Primary School, Holy Cross

The Big Match

As I first stepped on the court
My opponent stared at me
Like we were massive rivals
But now it was my turn to serve
Smash the ball as fast as flash
My opponent started sweating
As the sweat rolled down his face, he panicked.

James Dent (9)
Clent Parochial Primary School, Holy Cross

My Friend And I

Walk, talk, run, have fun
Draw and yawn, we're normal
That's what others say
But we don't care
We just play
I taught him pig Latin
He's my friend, Luke
My favourite one
Me and Luke every day.

Michael Porter (10)
Clent Parochial Primary School, Holy Cross

My Favourite Horse!

Barney is my heart horse
He is...

B eautiful
A mazing
R eady to go
N ever lets me down
E ver in my heart
Y ou are a superstar

He is a talented horse.

Lydia-Mai Drew (10)
Clent Parochial Primary School, Holy Cross

My Family And Me!

Generous and kind,
Reliable and friendly,
Mum, Dad, Nana,
Grandad, Grandma,
Cousins, Uncles, Aunties,
Other cousins and finally
My brothers and me
Doing fun things together
And forever in my head.

Harrison Dunn (9)
Clent Parochial Primary School, Holy Cross

Happy

My smile is so bright
It is the colour of the light
My colour is a dazzling shine
That brightens the night
I share my care
I heal my troubles
And still I'm as happy as can be
This is me!

Jessica Evans (10)
Clent Parochial Primary School, Holy Cross

When I'm Sad

When I'm sad I don't feel a lot
All I want is a hug, please
I don't want anything else
Just one simple hug, that's all
I only feel like crying.

Luke Steen (11)
Clent Parochial Primary School, Holy Cross

This Is Me

This is me
Music booming through my ears
Adventuring through trees
Racing through mountains
Diving into seas and rivers
Ziplining over rivers and lakes.

Reuben Mansell (11)
Clent Parochial Primary School, Holy Cross

This Is Me

I love travelling and exploring the world with
my family
I also love playing football and different sports
I like playing video games
I also love animals.

Dilan Tesse (9)

Clent Parochial Primary School, Holy Cross

Family

F orever

A nnoying

M adness

I dols

L oving

Y our family.

Jack Garner (9)

Clent Parochial Primary School, Holy Cross

Tennis

Tennis is my talent
But not my favourite sport
Every time I play
I am very distraught.

Aman Singh Virdee (9)

Clent Parochial Primary School, Holy Cross

And That's Me

F riendly, kind and smart
R ugby player heart
E veryone in my family is caring
Y our skills and my skills aren't for comparing
A cting makes me happy and that's me.

Freya Thomas (10)
Coulter Primary School, Coulter

Things To Describe Me

E nergetic all the time
L oves all things computers
I nto games a lot!

Eli MacNeilage (9)
Coulter Primary School, Coulter

My House

My house is not messy
Because I clean it every day
It is very fancy, come and see it any day
I play, I do my homework and I play at the park
But when I go, I make sure it's not too dark
It is very fun at home
Although I am very slow
This is the best house
Because it doesn't have a mouse
When I eat, I wash my hands and feet
But when I sleep
It feels like someone massaged me
Just before I pray, I say to myself
"Can't I do this every day?"

Japmann Singh (8)
Khalsa (VA) Primary School, Southall

The Khaneja Family

T stands for always travelling
H stands for always feeling happy
E stands for always enjoying life

K stands for knowledgeable
H stands for healthy
A stands for always accepting what happens
N stands for being noble at all costs
E stands for always encouraging each other
J stands for never being jealous
A stands for always agreeing with the family
S stands for never being selfish.

Sargun Khaneja (10)
Khalsa (VA) Primary School, Southall

Weather

Here comes winter
The snow is white like cotton candy
That is in December, January and February
Then comes spring
It's raining and the eggs are hatching
It gets warm in March, April and May
Later comes summer
The sun blazes through the window
It's as hot as a sauna in June, July and August
In autumn, the leaves are falling off the tree
It gets cold in September October and November.

Jujhar Khaneja (9)
Khalsa (VA) Primary School, Southall

All About Me Recipe

To make me, you will need:
11 pinches of kindness
12 pinches of positivity
2013 pinches of God's blessing

Each number represents me
Because these are my lucky numbers
And the date I was born
11/12/2013

My nickname is Japs
I call my dad Paps
And I call my mum Mams
Because she loves maps.

Japleen Kaur Kubar (9)
Khalsa (VA) Primary School, Southall

What Does It Take To Become An Author?

A ble to proudly read your writing
U nderstand questions and be able to share answers bravely
T o be confident
H ave a go, no matter what
O pen-minded at all times, never be afraid
R ead

This is what I want to be
When I get older
Writing is my passion.

Ashleen Khaneja (10)
Khalsa (VA) Primary School, Southall

Avimannat

Ambitious, kind, pretty
That is Avimannat
Mindful, attractive, noble
That is Avimannat
I am Avimannat

A mbitious
V ahiguru
I ntelligent
M indful
A ttractive
N eat
N oble
A chiever
T all.

Avimannat Kaur (9)
Khalsa (VA) Primary School, Southall

What Makes Me Smile?

What makes me smile
Doing PE with guile
That's what makes me smile

Playing with my sister
Makes her say, "Mister!
That's what makes me smile

I enjoy painting
And I love reading
That's what makes me smile.

Gurleen Kaur Aujla (10)
Khalsa (VA) Primary School, Southall

Cristiano Ronaldo CR7

When CR7 is on the pitch
It gives everyone a twitch
Everyone knows CR7 is the GOAT
They might as well get their coat
I saw him in real life
I had the time of my life
He is the best
And always a cut above the rest
CR7 is unstoppable.

Zorawar Birk Sidhu (7)
Khalsa (VA) Primary School, Southall

Arts And Crafts

I was doing my art
Painting a cart
But I only saw the sea
Drifting towards me
My brush was so lush
But my paint was no saint to me
I craft while I laughed
It's so good to be me.

Ganeev Kaur (10)
Khalsa (VA) Primary School, Southall

Football Fan

I'm a football fan
I love to be the man who gets to shout at refs
And get something off my chest
Whooping, whistling
Watching from the edge of my box
It's so much better than Roblox.

Kashmir Birk Sidhu (8)
Khalsa (VA) Primary School, Southall

Cricket

Cricket is a sport
Cricket is teamwork
Cricket is my craze
Cricket is my daddy's craze
Cricket is easy for me and my dad
My friend likes cricket
Everyone loves cricket, do you?

Tejvir Singh (9)
Khalsa (VA) Primary School, Southall

Rainbows

Rainbows are bright
Rainbows are light
When they come back
They are cool and right.

Japneet Kaur (8)
Khalsa (VA) Primary School, Southall

School

My friend is cool
She always goes to school
And she's not a fool.

Gurneet Kaur (8)
Khalsa (VA) Primary School, Southall

Me!

I am built of colours like yellow for happy and
blue for sad
Red for anger and purple for scared
And those colours make me

Yellow shows my happy and caring side
I am happy when people are happy
When people are caring, I'm caring
Yellow is me

Blue shows my sad, emotional side
I am sad when I find things hard and difficult
When I don't do things 100% I get sad
Blue is me

Red shows my anger and raging side
I am angry when people get louder and louder
And a ball of rage is inside of me
Red is me

Purple shows my scared and sensitive side
I get scared when I see my fears and horrors
Purple is me.

Lucy Sellwood (10)
Ladeside Primary School, Larbert

Halloween

H aunted houses and spooky nights
A mazing costumes to scare and fright
L aughter and fun for everyone
L ots of sweets for our tums
O oh, the ghosts and ghouls creep around
W itches, wizards, pirates and fairies join the crowd
E vening draws to a close and we all head home
E mpty our bags of sweets with gasps aloud
N ighttime falls and it's bedtime bound, to dream of pumpkins, games, laughter and the fun we had together.

Erin Smith (9)

Ladeside Primary School, Larbert

This Is Me

I am as wonderful as a wombat
Artistic as a monkey
I am as hungry as a hippo that's soon to be fed
I am lost in space at any time but people can
still see me
I'm a pro gamer like my dad
I'm as crazy as a cockatoo
As amazing as an armadillo
I am as happy as a bat flying about the night sky
I am as creative as a cat when it has a canvas
I'm as fantastic as a frog hiding in its hole.

Mya Snedden (11)

Ladeside Primary School, Larbert

This Is Me

I am as silly as a filly
I can be creative and intrigued
I can make jokes like a clown that is silly
I can be a star
I am as jolly as a frog
I can be inventive and enthusiastic
I can be extravagant
I can be as strong as a bolt
My life is as great, bright and bold as golden stars
I can be imaginative
This is me.

Alyssa Stirling (11)
Ladeside Primary School, Larbert

Me

A bowl full of creativeness
And a handful of quiet
Mix in some concentration
Creating my animations
A pinch of friendliness
And spoonful of shy
Mix into an amazing guy
Creating wavy curly hair
A full sprinkle of love
A spoonful of going to school
A pinch of playing video games
A bowl full of family life.

Mason Douglas (11)
Ladeside Primary School, Larbert

Unicorns

U nicorns are in my favourite stories

N ever do I get bored. My

I magination creates beautiful sparkly unicorns

C antering, galloping and having fun

O n so many adventures they have. I

R eally wish I could join them

N ext time, next chapter, next adventure. I hope I can.

Libby Smith (8)

Ladeside Primary School, Larbert

This Is Me!

T is for talking as I like to chat

Y is for why? As I'm inquisitive like that

L is for laughing. I enjoy having fun

E is for excitement when I tickle anyone

R is for respect as I like to follow the rules. It also stands for responsible when I use my grandpa's tools.

Tyler McDonald (11)

Ladeside Primary School, Larbert

Me

I 'm as playful as a kitten
S uper caring to all my friends
A s giggly as a hyena
B ashful when meeting new people
E xcited when going on a trip to the zoo
L ovingly waving to Zappy the Zebra
L aughing like a clown
A ll day long.

Isabella Kanzidis (13)
Ladeside Primary School, Larbert

Daisies

D aisies are amazing

A ngelika is my best friend

I like steak dipped in tomato sauce

S unshine is one of my favourite weathers

I like being in nature

E dinburgh is where my sister lives

S tarbucks is amazing.

Daisy Chipulu (9)
Ladeside Primary School, Larbert

This Is Me

First, start with a slice of mathematical knowledge
Next, add a drop of friendly
Afterwards, add some fun
Importantly, put in some loving big brother
Lastly, mix the ingredients to make me.

Sonny Gillie (11)
Ladeside Primary School, Larbert

Me

C reative like an astronaut
A nalytical like a professor
L ogical like an encyclopedia
I ntelligent like a computer
N avigating my way around my map of life.

Calin Cassidy (10)
Ladeside Primary School, Larbert

Home...

A haiku

The place I feel safe
A place where laughter blossoms
Where love begins... Home.

Olivia Bain (10)

Ladeside Primary School, Larbert

This Is Me

This is me
I am cool, I am smart
I like Lego and art
Each of my eyes is as brown as a chocolate ball
I'm good at basketball but I may not be tall

I like spiders
And Adidas sliders
I don't like rats
But I'm okay with cats

I don't like the wet
And I would like a pet
When I'm older I would like to be a rugby player
I like cake, especially a double-layer

My attitude is as good as a bunny
Everyone says I'm really funny
I like Santa
And orange Fanta

So this is me, I like playing with my friends
When I'm with them the fun never ends!

Ruaridh Rees (10)
Milesmark Primary School, Rumblingwell

This Is Me

To make me, you will need:
A very tiny bedroom with a side of teddies
A dash of creativity
A dash of brains
A dash of sassiness
2 marbles as green as grass
20 buckets of Taylor Swift music
1 bucket of clumsiness
5 spoonfuls of pencils
10 spoonfuls of paper

Now...
Add a very tiny bedroom with a side of teddies
Mix in a dash of brains
Whisk in a dash of creativity
Stir in 5 spoonfuls of pencils
Mix in 10 spoonfuls of paper
Add in 2 marbles as green as grass
Whisk in a dash of sassiness
Stir in a bucket of clumsiness
And finally, mix in 20 buckets of Taylor Swift music

Stir all together and bam, you've got me
This is me.

Ellie Fiona Cramb (10)
Milesmark Primary School, Rumblingwell

This Is Me

This is me, sometimes I am sad
And sometimes I am crazy mad
Mostly, I am good at maths
I love hot and steamy baths
I peculiarly like maths

I also like Nike
And I like to ride my bike

I also like to write
And get all my answers right

I like to use my right foot to play football
But I also use my left foot just as much
I have a good first touch
And I love to eat, *munch, munch!*

I also like to meet my friends
And I like it when school ends

I like light cotton wool
And also swimming in the pool
I love winning.

Munroe Candlish (10)
Milesmark Primary School, Rumblingwell

This Is Me

I am a small child
I am caring and wild
My favourite place to be is the football pitch
And when I kick the ball I know one day I will
be rich

I like eating chicken, roasted or fried
I like the colour turquoise, I think it looks divine
I have big brown eyes, they look like marbles
I am a fun football fan who supports Man United

I like it even though I am not good at it
I hope to improve and get through all of it
I like math and spelling makes me sad
I don't like writing, it gets me all mad.

Ilyas Razzaq (11)
Milesmark Primary School, Rumblingwell

This Is How To Make Me!

1 bucket of sport
2 cups of maths
3 pinches of music
3 pinches of kindness
4 cups of animals
A pinch of nature
2 spoons of being short
3 pinches of quirkiness

First, stir in a bucket of sport
Then pour in 2 cups of maths
Combine 3 pinches of music and kindness
Whisk together a love of animals
And add a pinch of nature
Sprinkle 3 pinches of quirkiness
And last but not least, add 2 pinches of being short
Bake until soft and bubbly
That is how you make me!

Maia Harker (10)

Milesmark Primary School, Rumblingwell

Pablo

Pablo, his name is as pleasant as can be
He is a wonder cat and that's all you need to see

He jumps along the couch all happy as can be
He sees his toy as dirty as can be

But that toy was smelly and dirty
Pablo was sad, he thought it was bad

But Pablo was as happy as a rainbow
When he sees his toy all pristine

There I see my little Pablo as small as can be
Biting his toy is all I can see.

Kerr Kelso (10)
Milesmark Primary School, Rumblingwell

This Is Me

I may be tall
But I can act as if I'm small
But I'm good at basketball
And I'm great at football

I really like Nike
But I do like to ride my bike
Sometimes I'm sad
But I know Hibs FC are bad

I like to swim in pools
And I am quite cool
My favourite animal is a seal
And, to me, they really appeal

I like colouring pens
And my gran has hens.

Rylie Smart (10)
Milesmark Primary School, Rumblingwell

This Is Me

B eing kind is my job

A n outstanding piper

G rowing as tall as a skyscraper is a wish of mine

P laying is a joy when my friends are around

I 'm as small as a mouse

P laying in the world bagpipe championship is a dream

E ven though I'm small, nothing can stop me.

Theerathan Halliday (11)
Milesmark Primary School, Rumblingwell

This Is Me!

F ast as lightning
O ften playing football on the bright green grass
O utstanding player
T all and speedy
B rown hair, darker than a bar of dark chocolate
A lways scoring goals
L oves Manchester United
L ifelong football lover.

Lucie Morrison (11)
Milesmark Primary School, Rumblingwell

This Is Me

I'm as kind as a guinea pig
I'm as caring as a dog
I'm as helpful as a pencil
I'm as fun as a bunny
I'm as fast as the Flash
I'm as successful as a famous person
I'm as sporty as a cheetah
And last but not least
I'm as smart as Einstein.

Connor Henderson (10)
Milesmark Primary School, Rumblingwell

Fat Cats

I love fat cats but not bats
Cats are cute, but more so when fat
Cats are cats, fat cats, silly belly cats
Mr Belly Cat's mischief is unbearably goofy
Also, his mouth is a bit toothy
This is the end, go be goofy.

Ben Fraser (10)
Milesmark Primary School, Rumblingwell

This Is Me

As warm as a soul
As slow as a frog
As small as a mouse
As kind as a tree
Sweet and kind, everything nice
Hot and cold are my favourite
Love or hate
When the wind hits my face, I feel joy
This is me.

Lailah Symon-Edwards (11)
Milesmark Primary School, Rumblingwell

This Is Me

This is me
I enjoy beating people in tennis
Some people would call me a menace
This is me
I am in a choir
My favourite song is 'Vampire'
This is me
I am very funny
And I am as sweet as honey.

Abigail Morton (10)
Milesmark Primary School, Rumblingwell

This Lilien

My eyes are blue like diamonds
I have blonde hair like vanilla
I am positive, clever, kind and helpful
My favourite food is pizza
I like to play games
I am a chatterbox
My favourite animals are bunnies because I
jump and like carrots
I am loyal to my brother
I am joyful
My favourite colours are white and brown
I try to face my fears
I am a superstar at tennis
I am good at swimming
I love cooking
I hate socks
I like the Eiffel Tower
I love dogs because they're adorable
I like blueberry frappe because it's delicious
I love autumn.

Lilien Somogyi (9)
Old Monkland Primary And Nursery School, Coatbridge

This Is Me

I am as kind as a nurse
My eyes are as blue as the ocean
My hair is blonde like ice cream
I am as pale as a ghost
I am as clingy as a cat
I am as skinny as a toothpick
I am as energetic as a rabbit
I am as creative as an artist
I am as fun as a monkey
I am as weird as a monkey
I have ears as big as a monkey
I am as fast as a car
I am as kind as a dog
I am as entertaining as a clown
I am as funny as a clown.

Freya Kay (9)
Old Monkland Primary And Nursery School, Coatbridge

I Am James Roy

I love the colour sky blue

A m good at art and being kind
M y eyes are blue like the sky

J am on pancakes is my favourite
A m always happy
M y favourite drink is tea
E lephants are my favourite animals
S ome of my friends are small but older than me

R oy is my surname
O ctopuses have eight legs
Y ou're the best

This is me.

James Roy (9)
Old Monkland Primary And Nursery School, Coatbridge

I Am Mollie

I love dogs and cats

A lways kind

M akes great art and crafts

M akes good drawings

O n Halloween, I am going to dress up as a zombie cheerleader

L ikes Stitch and Lilo

L oves animals

I n my house, I have a dog and his name is Barney

E ats crisps every day.

Mollie Brankin (9)

Old Monkland Primary And Nursery School, Coatbridge

I Am Amber

I am as kind as a princess

A m always happy on sunny days

M y cousin is turning one this month

A rt is something I am good at

M y favourite food is fish and chips

B ears are brown and fluffy

E yes as blue as the ocean

R ubble is my cat, cats are my favourite.

Amber Honeyman (8)

Old Monkland Primary And Nursery School, Coatbridge

This Is Me

T reat my sister well
H appiest when I'm playing football
I am a superstar goalkeeper
S o me and my friends will play

I have green marble eyes
S kins are in Fortnite

M y dogs are my favourite
E verything I do makes me happy.

Logan Cossutta (7)

Old Monkland Primary And Nursery School, Coatbridge

Rubie-Rose

R eally like pizza

U nited States for my holiday

B lue eyes like the sea

I like helping people

E ven if it's cleaning the house

R abbits are cute

O ceans have a lot of peace

S wimming is my sport

E milie is my sister.

Rubie-Rose Downes (8)
Old Monkland Primary And Nursery School, Coatbridge

I Am Oscar

I am as fast as lightning

A m a monkey
M y favourite sport is football

O lympics is the way I want to go
S port is my favourite
C ool cars I like
A s a footballer, I have to train
R ace cars are my favourite.

Oscar Brodie (9)
Old Monkland Primary And Nursery School, Coatbridge

Arabella

A m a rabbit

R abbits are my favourite

A m an animal that starts with R lover

B ella is one of my cousins

E nergy is what kids are made of

L ewly is my friend

L illy is my best friend

A m a paint lover.

Arabella Lyall (8)
Old Monkland Primary And Nursery School, Coatbridge

I Am Korey

K itKats taste like heaven

O h, how I love pizza

R angers are my favourite team. They really are the best

E very night I play Fortnite. I am as skilled as a sniper

Y ou know that I am mostly good but cheeky as a rascal.

Korey Love (8)

Old Monkland Primary And Nursery School, Coatbridge

I Am Freya

I love horses

A m a dog lover
M y eyes are as blue as the sea

F avourite colour is pink
R eally kind
E veryone is my friend
Y o-yos are my favourite
A mazing big cousin.

Freya Sanderson (8)
Old Monkland Primary And Nursery School, Coatbridge

This Is Me

I am as brave as a leopard
I am Lilly
I am wild
I am brave
I love Hedwig
I like Harry Potter
My BFF is Lilien, she is beautiful
My second name is Renee
I try to be brave
I love Maine Coon cats
I love Husky dogs.

Lilly Gardiner (9)
Old Monkland Primary And Nursery School, Coatbridge

I Am Cody

I am the fastest in my class

A m a monkey
M y favourite colour is red

C ody is who I am
O ranges I like
D ribbling the ball every day
Y ou can be any character in my game.

Cody Hillan (8)
Old Monkland Primary And Nursery School, Coatbridge

I Am Lewis

I am good at football
I am as small as a baby monkey
I am lightning-fast in football boots
I play on the right wing and sometimes goalkeeper
I live in Coatbridge
Jaffa Cakes are my favourite
I am great at dribbling balls.

Lewis Calder (8)
Old Monkland Primary And Nursery School, Coatbridge

What I Am Good At

I like to run
I also have fun in the sun
My favourite colour is blue
The stars shine like it's all they know how to do
Gymnastics is my sport
I am good at handstands
I can even do them in the sand.

Lorena Small (9)

Old Monkland Primary And Nursery School, Coatbridge

About Myself

I like my PS4
I like The Last Of Us
I like Fortnite
I like school
I like Harry Potter
I like my phone
I like my tablet
I like football.

Josh Lawrie (8)
Old Monkland Primary And Nursery School, Coatbridge

How To Make Me

To create me, you will need:
A bottle of hugs
A cupful of friendship
A handful of books
4 jugs of imagination
8 pints of maturity

How to make:
First, you need to get a big pot
Pour in 8 pints of maturity
Mix with a cup of friendship and pat until bubbly
Next, add a handful of books
Sprinkle in all of the 4 jugs of imagination,
carefully, a bit at a time
If you pour the jugs too quickly it will go lumpy
Mix all the ingredients and carry on pouring until
all the imagination is gone
Finally, put in the oven for an hour
Or until a skewer can come out clean
Then shape into a slug and voila
You have made me!

Cecily Smith (7)
RGS Dodderhill School, Droitwich Spa

The Pieces Of Me

What makes me my unique mosaic?
When I think of all the things and people that
make me what I am
My eyes and heart smile with joy

My grandad Mike gifted me with a dollop of
creativity and imagination
My grandad Liam blessed me with a swirl of
wisdom and kindness
My daddy equipped me with a jar full of humour
and logic
My mummy provided me with a cup of gentleness
and nurturing
My little sister gave me a spoonful of laughter
and patience
My friends present me with a splash of playfulness
and support
The books that I read ignite a bottle full of
brilliance and inspiration
My teachers show me, in abundance, the path of
life and where it can take me

Each of these is a swirl of lively bright unique vibrant colours
Everything adds up to love and this creates a mosaic of me

This is me!

Violet Craze (9)
RGS Dodderhill School, Droitwich Spa

Full Of Joy

To create me, you will need:
A blob of Blu-Tac
A large dollop of creativity
A box of Pokémon
A love of koalas
A cupboard of flexibility
A cup of Australia
A house of dogs
A box of tortoises
A baby elephant
A hat of love
A car of friendship

Instructions:
Mix the blob of Blu-Tac and add a large dollop of creativity
Mix it all together
Throw in a box of Pokémon and stir in a love of koalas
Dump in a cupboard of flexibility
Sieve a cup of Australia and a house of dogs

With a box of tortoises and a sprinkle of
baby elephant
Add a hat of love and lastly, a car of friendship
Cook for fifteen minutes and you have it
This is me, full of joy.

Olivia Lloyd-Allum (10)
RGS Dodderhill School, Droitwich Spa

Lemon Cake Me

To create me, you will need:
100g of rugby
A gallon of humour
200g of martial art
A blob of craziness
A dash of shyness
100g of bravery
A gallon of journey
1000g of sport

Now you need to:
Add a dash of shyness into a large mixing bowl
Then gradually pour in a gallon of journey
Now add 100g of bravery and 100g of rugby
Next, sieve 1000g of sport
Now sprinkle in 200g of martial art
Crack in a blob of craziness after a gallon
of humour
Next, heat your oven to 180°

Bake for twenty minutes
When ready, put on the icing

This is me!

Lucy Wainwright (9)
RGS Dodderhill School, Droitwich Spa

A Recipe To Make Me

To make me:
Get a large bowl and add 500g of fun
Next, mix in a pint of friendship
Toss in a handful of cheekiness
Then pour in a bottle of imagination
Whisk in a spoonful of creativity
Then swirl in a scoop of independence
Next, fold in a jug full of love
Then knead in a large glug of pinkness
Leave it on the side for fifteen minute
Then sprinkle a dollop of Blu-Tac in
Next, mould a jug of baby animal love
Finally, in a separate bowl, stir in a pinch
of freckles,
A pint of gymnastics and a jug of games
Once cool, ice with a dollop of smiles and voila
You've made me!

Lola Herriotts (8)
RGS Dodderhill School, Droitwich Spa

A Recipe About Me

First, add a love of piano
Next, shake a gallon of friendship
After, toss in a pinch of spiky hair
Then mix some love of animals
After that, whisk in 500g of cheekiness
Then toss in 1000g of smiles
After, knead in a lot of fun
Then add a load of art
Toss in some naughtiness
Then add a bit of love to sprinkle on top
For extra taste, mix some love of trampolining
Finally, add some respect on top
There you have made me
So put in the oven for forty-five minutes
And there you go, you have made me!

Alby White (8)
RGS Dodderhill School, Droitwich Spa

How To Make Me!

To create me, you will need:
A jug of friendship
A cup of love
A dash of craziness
A pinch of dogs
A gallon of humour
A hint of joy
A glass of smiles
A hint of kindness
A cup of sports

Now you need to:
Get a bowl of happy and set the oven to 188°
Add the glass of smiles
Mix the gallon of humour
Melt the cup of sports and then add it
Sieve in a hint of joy, a pinch of dogs and a jug of friendship
Mix very firmly
Put in the oven for five minutes

Let it cool down and add a hint of kindness and
a cup of love
This is me!

Eloise Hogwood (9)
RGS Dodderhill School, Droitwich Spa

My Recipe Poem

To create me, you will need:
A handful of friendship
A bottle of foxes
A dash of fun
A handful of artistic
A teaspoon of door-holding
A bowl of kindness
A pinch of honesty
A bowl of humour

Now you need to:
Pour in a bowl of kindness
Mix with a pinch of honesty
Pour in a teaspoon of door-holding
Add a bowl of humour
Mix with a bottle of foxes with a handful
of friendship
Add a dash of fun
And a handful of artistic skills
Cook for three minutes
This is me!

Isabella Chance (9)
RGS Dodderhill School, Droitwich Spa

Me

To create me, you will need:
A sprinkle of kindness
A hint of fun
A spoonful of funniness
A drop of horse love
A large scoop of love for Jasper and Rupert
A bowl full of snake love

Now you need to:
First, get a bowl full of snake love
Then quickly stir in a drop of horse love
After that, add a hint of fun
Next, throw in a large scoop of love for Jasper
and Rupert
Then put the oven on for half an hour
Next, leave it to cool
After that, sprinkle on some kindness
Enjoy!

Isabella Gough (9)
RGS Dodderhill School, Droitwich Spa

What Makes Me Happy

Swings and monkey bars give me delight
When the golden sun shines bright
One dog playing with a ball
No frowning, not at all
What makes me happy is the time of joy
Playing and chatting everywhere
Playing games and running about
We'll play on the trampoline with no doubt
Talking about secret things
All the things that make me grin
What makes me happy is the time of joy
Playing and chatting everywhere
Oh, these things as you see
Fill me up with glee
And that is what makes me happy.

Grace Hogwood (9)
RGS Dodderhill School, Droitwich Spa

This Is Me

To create me, you will need:
A pinch of loveliness
A splash of kindness
A sprinkle of enjoyment
5lb of generosity
A big dash of love

Now you need to:
Add a pinch of loveliness
Mix in a sprinkle of enjoyment
After that, you need to put in a splash of kindness
and 5lb of generosity
Once you have done that, you need to put the last
ingredient in which is a big dash of love
Stir well and put in the oven
Now you have a 'This Is Me' cake.

Lorianna Mason (9)
RGS Dodderhill School, Droitwich Spa

A Recipe Poem

To create me, you will need:
A sprinkle of craziness
A pinch of kindness
A bottle of mindfulness
A great big smile
A sprinkle of independence
A pepperoni pizza
Cook!

After it's cooked
Add a dash of chocolate
A spoonful of Roblox
Some essence of Pokémon
Mix it all together for 100 hours
Then add a final touch of monkey.

This is me!

Joseph Spencer (10)
RGS Dodderhill School, Droitwich Spa

A Recipe To Make Me

First, put in a cup of creativity
Then add the strong spice of imagination
Next, whisk in some cat love
After that, add a blob of kindness and the love
of a kind sister
Don't forget the handful of funny
Stir them up and put them in the barrel of
cheeky and naughtiness
Cook them up and you have made me!

Madeleine Sisson (8)
RGS Dodderhill School, Droitwich Spa

A Recipe To Make Me

First, you will need to add 3 scoops of kindness
Mix in a handful of creativity
Next, pour in a bottle of hugs
Add a dash of fun
Stir in a sprinkle of animals in a bowl
After that, add a jugful of imagination
Tip the bowl out and spread the nature on a tray
Then put it in the oven until it is nice and golden.

Lily Spencer (7)
RGS Dodderhill School, Droitwich Spa

This Is Me!

To create me, you will need:
A handful of gamer
A gallon of craziness
A sprinkle of humour
A pint of mischievousness

Now you need to:
Mix a big handful of Roblox
Add a dash of Domino's pizza
Stir in a big bunch of hugs
This is me!

James Spencer (10)
RGS Dodderhill School, Droitwich Spa

A Recipe To Make Me

First, add a bottle of kindness
Next, pour in a large glug of creativity
Then shake in a wheelbarrow full of arachnids
Afterwards, add a pinch of polka-dot freckles
Pop in a bowlful of foxes
Add a dollop of cheekiness
And voila! You have made me!

Cameron Hollingworth (7)
RGS Dodderhill School, Droitwich Spa

A Recipe To Make Me

First, add a spoonful of books
Then put in a sprinkle of art
Add a big dollop of kindness
Finally, add 500g of imagination
Put in the oven for an hour
Once cooled, add a pinch of singing and games.

Edie Banyard (7)
RGS Dodderhill School, Droitwich Spa

Winter Days

When it's winter and when it's cold
I fasten up my laces, all fluffy and warm

I opened my door and what did I see?
All of the snowflakes, fluttering around me

I built a snowman, all white and cold
I looked up at the sky and loads of stories it told

My lips were all rosy and cosy
My hair was brown and crisp

I made a snow angel
And I added a manger to my tree

I looked at the tree, my hands were warm
Welcoming and a helper

I go back home to see my dog
He was all fluffy and cosy
Like my teddy, Mosy

My eyes always glitter when my family
comes down
I would never give a single frown

My family are so important to me
It makes me get filled with glee

So when I went into the lounge what did I see?
Santa's left so many presents for me! Yippee!

This is me.

Annelle Campbell (8)
St Mary's Catholic Voluntary Academy, Marple Bridge

Iris

I am Iris

R eading is my passion

I love art but it is rather hard

S ewing is fun, I enjoy it very much

I love animals especially dogs because I have one

S hooting stars remind me of me because I shoot across the dance floor

A teacher is what I wish to be because I love to read and write

M y family and friends are really important to me. I love them with all my heart even though they annoy me

A star is what I wish to be as bright as the sun

Z ipwires are really fun. It feels like being put into a car with no control

I love Aeriel hoop, it is so fun twirling and whirling high in the sky

N othing makes me as happy as coming home from a busy day at school, putting my feet up and seeing my family

G rounding is really fun, it calms me down when I need it.

Iris Mulryan (9)
St Mary's Catholic Voluntary Academy, Marple Bridge

The Amazing Claridge

I am me, I am me
I love pugs, my faves are the babies
I am me
I like maths and sport
My fave subject is art
I love art
I am me, I am me
Teachers are so kind
The assistants just as much
I love my family, they are so cool
I am me
I have two cats, they are not very old
My nanna has cats just like me
One of them is hungry and one of them sleeps
I am me
Otters! I love otters
But don't forget that cats are my fave
I am me
Happy, helpful, calm
I can be all the feelings
I am me

My eyes are precious, coloured raindrops
I am me
A wonder of the universe
I am me
I love everyone and everything
I am cool, in fact, I'm cooler than everyone
I am me
I love black
I am me.

Rain Claridge (8)
St Mary's Catholic Voluntary Academy, Marple Bridge

Sports And Games For Me

I am a fantastic footballer
A super striker with a big heart

I am a swimming superstar, as fast as a shark
With super speed and a passionate part

I'm very good at video games
Minecraft is for me

My friends play great games with me
And they always make me happy

Board games are really fun
But when I lose I give myself a bruise

When I see people alone and sad
It makes me feel bad

I get a lot of games to play on television
But when I sit on a slide I always have pride
And a bit of friction

I always like taking part
In doing art

Games are always fun for me
Because I go running wild and free

This is a poem about me.

Callum Deegan (9)
St Mary's Catholic Voluntary Academy, Marple Bridge

Best Things About Me

B right and colourful is how I make my art
E ggs I love but not scrambled, yuck
S inging is my best thing
T he thing I like is my family, they are so kind and loving

T he thing I like to do is play games all day
H appy, helpful, I love school
I love pets, they are so cute and fluffy
N o one can break me up from my friends
G reat and fast as a rapid blue sea
S un, sun, you are warm. I wish you were here all day

A dog is my favourite pet because it is cute
B FFs are Kitty, Maria and Rain
O h, my favourite food is pizza
U mbrella, I don't want to use. I like the rain
T he end of my poem.

Margot Emery (7)
St Mary's Catholic Voluntary Academy, Marple Bridge

This Is Me

T he world is my oyster

H olidays make me happier

I n my home, I have a dog

S wizzle, she leaps like a frog

I nterested in reading, writing and English

S eas inspire me with the fish

M y Sundays are spent playing rugby for Marple

E yes of mine are ocean-like marbles

This is me, the dog-loving rugby player
Who my hooligan friends have come to love

I love pandas, I love dogs, I love bats, I love frogs
I love my mum, my dad, my brother, he's a lad
I love loud, I love quiet, I make peace, I make a riot
I love light, I love dark because they're both part of
my heart
Now that's my story made up of glory.

Herbie Keene (10)

St Mary's Catholic Voluntary Academy, Marple Bridge

Me, Glorious Me

I like Eurovision 2023
Those are my favourite songs as you can see
Sometimes I'm happy, sometimes I'm sad
Sometimes I'm good, sometimes I'm bad

My favourite colour is blue
But I like green too
I like my brothers even though they are cheeky
I don't know how they act so quietly and so meekly

My family go on holiday every year
We always go to Italy and the pizzeria
My dad has a twin and three brothers
One of my aunties has become a mother

I was diagnosed with coeliac disease when
I was two
Now I am class captain so I can boss you
I have a cat and his name is Rory
He likes to snuggle whilst I tell him a story
This is me.

Lucia Tognarelli (8)
St Mary's Catholic Voluntary Academy, Marple Bridge

This Is Me!

History I love
My favourite symbol is a dove
Stories are my speciality
A way to escape from reality
Eating sweets, an extreme sport
One too many and your face will contort
Sing this really low
All my friends, here we go
Olivia, Rebecca, Jemima
Sing this a little big higher
Millie, Ella, Judy
If I miss you I'm not being rudy
Sofia, Gracie, Izzy
Sing this faster, you'll get dizzy
Aoife, Anna, Sadie
Anna likes really cute babies
And before I go
I really must say
We're all special in our own unique way.

Inès Vibert
St Mary's Catholic Voluntary Academy, Marple Bridge

The Penguin Lover

I am a penguin lover as lovely as can be
My hair is like dirt but really brown
Sometimes I get a red cut on my knee
Don't ask me what my type of food is
It's pizza and couscous
Please don't say unkind words to a penguin lover
Or you will get the death stare
And you do not want to see the death stare
Do you understand?
Please, please give me a penguin
My eyes are as blue as the sparkling ocean
I'm more of a rockstar type of person
My skin is quite peachy and dark
Never ever kill a penguin or you are dead!

Kitty Groarke-Booth (7)
St Mary's Catholic Voluntary Academy, Marple Bridge

Trains

T rains are brilliant, trains are great

R acing along tracks and hauling freight;

A round the world they zoom around, taking people homeward-bound;

I ngeniously designed with a billowing funnel and pistons and wheels to fly through tunnels;

N othing can compare to Britain's trains: we have the Rocket, the first in the race and maybe soon, we'll make one that flies to space;

S o this sums up my brief talk on trains and transport: so enjoy a ride but pay for your ticket for you may get caught.

Jacob Jensen (11)

St Mary's Catholic Voluntary Academy, Marple Bridge

This Is Me

T eaching myself how to do stuff

H obbies are my favourite thing, I like them

I like dogs and my friend likes cats. Animals are my favourite

S printing at a thousand miles per hour. I am the fastest thing in the world

I 'm called Leo and my birthday is in October so I am creepy

S aying kind things makes me smile so be kind and I will be kind too

M y favourite place is Spain because I like the food

E xercise is good for you, I love it and my heart does too.

Leo Brown (7)

St Mary's Catholic Voluntary Academy, Marple Bridge

This Is Me, Ike!

This is me, I'm nine
I'm a shining light with footy boots on my feet
And like the shine my car gives me

"You have a good personality"
Says my mum and I agree

I like VR and tech
Give me a game and I'll make it on scratch

I really like cars like my dad's Porsche
It's fun to drive but not for long

My days are just VR and also some tech
Then I'll have dinner and kick in my net
And then I'll go to bed

Everyone loves Ike.

Isaac Jones (9)
St Mary's Catholic Voluntary Academy, Marple Bridge

This Is Me

After a long day of football
The sweat is dripping
The Astro picks who is winning
My life is about the ball
I don't like the weather when the rain falls
Because it could cancel the great football
I am running high
I'll make you smile even when flying in the sky
I love spicy fried chicken wings
But my greedy axolotl
Would probably want to nibble the wings
Family is also incredibly great
And finally, if anyone is mean
My friends will clean up the scene
This is me.

Jonah Young (10)
St Mary's Catholic Voluntary Academy, Marple Bridge

This Is Me

My dogs are as skinny as a pencil
But I love them very much
My cat is as fat as a rat

I am a super striker
And I am number eleven
I play for Stockport County Academy
And it's a blast

I'm as brave as a bear
And as fierce as a fire-breathing dragon

I love baking cakes with my grandma
And building Lego with my wonderful dad

Sailing across Windermere
And the ocean with my family
I love water skiing and loving my life.

Anya Butler (10)
St Mary's Catholic Voluntary Academy, Marple Bridge

The Cool Poem

L oving to my family and friends
U nbeatable at the aerial hoop
C olourful is my personality
I want my job to be as a hairdresser
A t school, I am always sensible

I have two rabbits named Nibbles and Hops
S uper duper funny when someone is sad

C aring when someone is hurt
O n task when doing work
O lives are delicious and make me different
L ook carefully if my spelling is wrong.

Lucia Gianferrari (8)
St Mary's Catholic Voluntary Academy, Marple Bridge

This Is Me

I jump, I sprint all over the place
Whether high or long
I've got it all covered

I scream, I shout
I mess about
All over and around
I don't know why they get irate

I love and like chocolate and sweets
They taste very much like fire

I shoot and kick all over the place
And don't need to hope that it goes in
That's where the fun begins

I play with my friends and mess about
All we do is chill out.

Isaac Chrippes (10)

St Mary's Catholic Voluntary Academy, Marple Bridge

All About James

J umping around, I'm a frog
A s I walk around
M y eyes are always a seamless planet
E verything I do is as good as a gold medal
S ometimes I am a star at maths

T his is me, who is a cheetah in my trainers
O utdoor activities are exciting
L ovely singing I do
L onely waiting at the bus stop
E ager for chocolate, I'm not really hungry
Y ou should be as good as me.

James Tolley (7)
St Mary's Catholic Voluntary Academy, Marple Bridge

I Love Dogs!

I love dogs, I love dogs so much. They are

L ovely and fluffy. They are kind and cuddly

O ut of all the dogs in the world, I love

V ery much is the Daschunds

E verything about them is cute and cuddly

D o you have a dog? I love dogs so very much

O ver every dog in the world, I like Daschunds. They are

G ood and cute and cuddly all the time but

S ometimes they are as cheeky as a mouse.

Florence Royle (7)
St Mary's Catholic Voluntary Academy, Marple Bridge

All About Me!

Some of my favourite animals are elephants, goats and dogs but I like them all
My favourite thing to wear on my head is a woolly hat, of course
I am a greedy pizza stealer and a McDonald's stealer
Time to read, I am a bookworm, a seriously wiggly worm
Harry Potter is my favourite but wait
I mean Harry Potter and The Prisoner Of Azkaban
Yellow and Blue are my favourite colours
Mix them together and you make green.

Amelia Smith (7)

St Mary's Catholic Voluntary Academy, Marple Bridge

How To Make Me

To make me, you will need:
KFC
Blonde hair
A football
Blue eyes
Red
My friends
A pot and spoon

The order to make me:
Get the pot out and put KFC in it
Take a pinch of blonde hair and put it in the pot
Throw a football into the pop
Take out a blue eye and put it in the pot
Pour red paint into the pot
Put my friends in there
Stir it with a spoon
And you have me!

Harry Woodhead (8)
St Mary's Catholic Voluntary Academy, Marple Bridge

Jack

I am good at karate
I love animals
I love my friends
I am kind
I like playing with toys
I have five friends
I sit next to my friends every day
My favourite animal is a gecko
I am kind to my sister
I am kind to my nanna's dog
I am kind to my aunty's dog
I love my sister
I love my mummy
I love my daddy
I have three friends at karate
I am kind to my grandparents.

Jack Callaghan (6)
St Mary's Catholic Voluntary Academy, Marple Bridge

The Amazing Lydia

T his is me. I am a complete bookworm

H aving fun is the best when I get to play with my friends

I am a lion, brave and strong

S ee me run as fast as a cheetah

I am a super striker and really good in goal

S loths are the best in the world

M ango is the best food ever

E ven though I really love sloths, I love my family two times as much.

Lydia Crosthwaite (7)
St Mary's Catholic Voluntary Academy, Marple Bridge

This Is Me

I am as elegant as an elephant
I am fun like a hot cross bun who can run
I am as smart as a Pop-Tart
I am as funny as a luxurious little bunny
Sometimes I cut my knees
Yet I still dislike peas and bees
I am very sweet and I like to eat
If you call, I will play football
Running past, I'm quite fast
I like to do art, and draw body parts
I like monkeys, because they are funky.

Judy Mylrea (10)
St Mary's Catholic Voluntary Academy, Marple Bridge

This Is Me

I am a sports lover
I am a fast runner
I am a science lover
I am a great footballer
I am a food connoisseur
I am an animal lover
I have two dogs and two cats
I am a twin
Although sometimes we squabble
My family has to be here
And, of course, my best mates
Although I like to run, jump and swim
I still love a good burger
And all of that is the definition of me.

Orry Mylrea (10)
St Mary's Catholic Voluntary Academy, Marple Bridge

This Is Me!

I am funny, busy, kind
Plus a great big mind
English is my passion
I also quite like fashion
I go to St Mary's school
And also the girls do rule
My dog, Josie, has died
And sometimes I have lied
I am a good sister
And I think I mainly miss her
I am a good reader
Though I'm a really bad weaver
Born in 2014
Thought I was quite keen
This is me!

Florence Harrison (8)
St Mary's Catholic Voluntary Academy, Marple Bridge

Lovely Lois

L over of beautiful animals

O ver the moon when drawing

V ery happy when reading books

E very day I love to play

L ovely songs I love listening to

Y es, I love gymnastics and dancing

L ove board games and my friends

O n top of the world

I s the best place for me

S ee me with my friends

I am Lois.

Lois Tomlinson (8)

St Mary's Catholic Voluntary Academy, Marple Bridge

This Is Me

I am Austin
I love cats and dogs
I can't think which is my favourite
I've just found out that I like cats more than dogs
You've forgotten my name? How?
My name is Austin
I have a passion for pizza
I love swimming
I'm the best swimmer
I like it when the sun beams in the sky
My face is a clock
A cat is in my house
This is me.

Austin Gallogly-Frame (6)

St Mary's Catholic Voluntary Academy, Marple Bridge

Super Annie-Mae

This is me and what I am like
My hair is as yellow as a sunflower
I have blue eyes like the sea
I would like to be a horse trainer
I have a nice super mum and dad
And a super niece called Betty
I have a super dog called pompom
I am as speedy as a cat
I have a fish that is as long as a giant
lying on the floor
My rabbit is as fluffy as a pompom.

Annie-Mae Field (7)
St Mary's Catholic Voluntary Academy, Marple Bridge

Where's My Teddy Penguin?

What shall we play?
I know what to play, hide-and-seek
I will get going, go and hide
One, two, three, four, five
I am coming
Where's my teddy?
Playtime dog, can you help me find it?
Noo! I know he is hiding
Oh, there you are!
It is time to catch TV, Penguin
This is my penguin
I like you, Penguin
I think it is penguin time.

Pauric Beetham (6)
St Mary's Catholic Voluntary Academy, Marple Bridge

My Favourite Things

I love painting the garden from top to bottom
It helps me look at the garden when it's rainy
I am a sweet swimmer
When I come back my dog brings me a toy to
play fetch
I love dogs
I am a superstar singer
When it has stopped raining I come out to
sunbathe
Then I come back in and play Twister with
my dog
He is a superstar.

Niamh Barlow (7)
St Mary's Catholic Voluntary Academy, Marple Bridge

This Is Me!

I have a cool dog
Who climbs over a log
I have a gerbil who I love
My favourite bird is a dove
I don't have any money
And I hate runny honey
I make a Christmas list
And I wrote a fairy wish
I love my family, no matter what
My dog has a black dot
My dog is one
And I should have won
This is me.

Aoife Wood

St Mary's Catholic Voluntary Academy, Marple Bridge

Brilliant George

I am a great tackler when I have my boots
I am fantastic at my swimming
I am a brilliant horse rider
I am a rugby player
I have eyes as dark as a cave
I am a superstar bookworm
I have a passion for fish and chips
I love dogs
I love their soft fur
I am the best tree climber
I am so fast I can beat a hound.

George Percy (6)
St Mary's Catholic Voluntary Academy, Marple Bridge

My Favourite Animal

When up in the trees
Life is a breeze
When down on the ground
My home can't be found

I'm ever so cute
With orange fur like the fruit
I can sometimes be crazy
But mostly I'm lazy

Lying in the sun
I find really fun
Climbing is my lifestyle
One look at me will make you smile.

Ella Crosthwaite (10)
St Mary's Catholic Voluntary Academy, Marple Bridge

This Is Me

I am as strong as a tiger
I have ocean-blue eyes
I am as fast as a cheetah
I am a superstar footballer
I love animals, my favourite is Sonny
I am as kind as a nurse
I am as rich as a king
I am a superstar swimmer
I am a bookworm
I have a passion for pizza
I am a fantastic footballer
This is me.

Jonah Wood (6)

St Mary's Catholic Voluntary Academy, Marple Bridge

Amazing Annie

T he smell of cheesy pasta is the best smell
H i, I love koalas and pandas
I am a bookworm and I love books
S easide is my favourite place to be

I have green marble eyes
S unflower yellow hair

M y favourite season is winter
E very day is my favourite.

Annie Thompson (6)
St Mary's Catholic Voluntary Academy, Marple Bridge

This Is Me

Football is fun
But the Astro is where the real fun begins
Running down the wing with their ankles in
my pocket
While my studs are ready to pounce
But at the same time, my jokes are ready
to pounce
My size may be small but my mischief is high
If anyone is mean I have my mates to clean
up the scene.

Joe Buckley (10)

St Mary's Catholic Voluntary Academy, Marple Bridge

Amazing Animals!

A mazing hamsters running so fast
N aughty cats sneaking all around
I n the jungle, you can find speedy cheetahs
M ind-blowing amazing bookworms, just like me
A mazing flamingoes flying up high
L ovely animals but maybe not super snakes
S illy salamanders are lots of fun.

Maria Hockey (7)

St Mary's Catholic Voluntary Academy, Marple Bridge

Amazing Daniel Lee

T uesday is the best day of the week
H orses are my favourite animal
I am a great goalkeeper
S easide is my best thing

I love the Mario teddies
S is my favourite letter

M an City are the best team in the world
E njoys playing with my brother.

Daniel Lee (7)
St Mary's Catholic Voluntary Academy, Marple Bridge

This Is Me

T he park is my favourite place to be
H i, my name is Nicco the Brave
I am a footballer
S upper is my favourite time of day

I love playing football
S uperstar swimmer

M an United are the best team in the world
E njoys playing on the Nintendo.

Nicco Tognarelli (6)
St Mary's Catholic Voluntary Academy, Marple Bridge

Fantastic Lottie

I am good at looking after animals
My favourite is a rabbit
I am as kind as a butterfly
I will not hurt you
I am a super swimmer
I am as speedy as a speedboat
My hair is as brown as a chocolate bar
I am a dazzling dancer
I have a passion for pasta
My eyes are as blue as the sea
This is me.

Lottie Mayers (6)
St Mary's Catholic Voluntary Academy, Marple Bridge

My Dog

My dog is as friendly as the sun
Her tears are little puddles
She is a whizzing cheetah
Sometimes she is a cheeky monkey
She can have so much fun
I have to give her a bun
She loves to sniff a bum
Her eyes are black rolling marbles
Her bark is as loud as thunder
She snores as quietly as a mouse.

George Drake (7)
St Mary's Catholic Voluntary Academy, Marple Bridge

All About Me

W hen I wake up, I start my day

I like to play Fortnite to start the day

L ater, I played football with my dad and scored a goal

L unch comes next and I like pizza

I drink some Pepsi and watch TV

A fter that, I brush my teeth

M y day is over when I close my eyes.

William Mayers (8)
St Mary's Catholic Voluntary Academy, Marple Bridge

This Is Me

T he holiday is Paris for me
H elp with some flags, ask me
I am a whizz at my times tables
S ee the best show

I adore Knights of the Zodiac
S et a nice sunset

M y eyes are as brown as mud
E very Pokémon card is the best.

Mathieu Vibert (7)
St Mary's Catholic Voluntary Academy, Marple Bridge

I Am Me

I am a dolphin in the ocean
I am like a sloth at maths

Anything to do with foxes, that's me
I am as calm as a fox

My hair is chocolate brown
I hate spicy food

My eyes are like two earths in drops
I love everything about foxes
They are fluffy and adorable.

Annabelle Tsopanou (7)
St Mary's Catholic Voluntary Academy, Marple Bridge

This Is Me

Just imagine your own world, however, you like
Flying cats, zooming pigs and even a floating bike
Stuff made of chocolate, giant sweets and even
upturned seats
Enormous trees, tiny bees, never-ending seas
Fishing out sharks, million-paged books,
rainbow marks
What world will you imagine?

Olivia Smiley
St Mary's Catholic Voluntary Academy, Marple Bridge

Grace

G iraffes are my favourite animal forever and ever

R acing for medals as I race for my team

A ll of my friends are nice but my best friend is Florence F

C ats and kittens, how much more cute can they be?

E nding a school day, having a nice tea to have a nice dream.

Grace Walker (7)

St Mary's Catholic Voluntary Academy, Marple Bridge

Danny Dan

I am a bookworm when it comes to reading
I am a fantastic footballer
My hair is as yellow as a sunflower
I love animals and a dog is my favourite
I have eyes as brown as a tree's dead leaves
I love my friends and family
I have a passion for pizza
I am a superstar swimmer.

Daniel Purrier (6)

St Mary's Catholic Voluntary Academy, Marple Bridge

The Winnie Rap!

I got a dog, her name is Winnie
She likes to eat stuff from the binny
She knows all the tricks, she's got Nike kicks
She drinks toilet water, she likes to slaughter
She's super fast, she'll be running past
After walks, we need a rest
My amazing dog really is the best.

Tom Wiedemann (10)
St Mary's Catholic Voluntary Academy, Marple Bridge

This Is Me

To make me, you will need:
1 million pounds of happiness
1 teaspoon of sadness
5 teaspoons of bravery
1 gallon of blood
All of the organs of the human body

Now you need love
And put to bed at 3am
I will pop out
And you will have me!

This is me.

Evan Freeman (8)
St Mary's Catholic Voluntary Academy, Marple Bridge

James

I am a terrific tennis player
I am a lover of animals
My favourite is an armadillo
I am a bookworm
I have a passion for pasta
I am going to be a fireman
I am as small as a pony
I am a world lover
My eyes are as brown as mud
My hair is as brown as a wolf.

James Camm (6)
St Mary's Catholic Voluntary Academy, Marple Bridge

This Is Me!

T he youngest girl in my family
H elp people who need it
I n and out I'm amazing
S port is my passion

I am a fantastic runner
S upport people whenever

M ake people smile
E very day I do my thing.

Lucy Carter (9)

St Mary's Catholic Voluntary Academy, Marple Bridge

Amazing Harry

I am a sea swimmer
I am the fastest in football
I love pizzas
If I could I would eat them all
I love dogs
I have lots of friends
I love Pokémon
I love McDonald's
The smell of pizza is the best smell for me
I love Captain Underpants.

Harry Wiedemann (7)
St Mary's Catholic Voluntary Academy, Marple Bridge

This Is Me

C aring and kind describe me
A cting is something I like to do
I will be a drama star
T he animal I adore is the hamster
L oving and adoring also describe me
I love gymnastics above all
N ow that describes me.

Caitlin Camm (8)

St Mary's Catholic Voluntary Academy, Marple Bridge

This Is Me

T hank you for my friends
H elpful in every way
I like dogs
S wimming is my thing

I like gymnastics
S uper sister

M ax and Bruno are my rabbits
E njoy playing with Rosa and Florence.

Lily Sharrocks (8)
St Mary's Catholic Voluntary Academy, Marple Bridge

This Is Me

Fashion is my passion
I love to design and create
Until it is late
Gucci is my favourite
Sometimes I crave it.

F un
A mazing
S tylish
H appy
I n the trend
O n point
N ew trend.

Sofia Evans
St Mary's Catholic Voluntary Academy, Marple Bridge

This Is Me

I run the cross-country as fast as a cheetah
Running 100 miles an hour
I am kind like my friends at school
I like to help people
My eyes are the colour blue
Barking, miaowing and squeaking
Is what you will hear at my house
I am an animal lover.

Finley Wass (7)
St Mary's Catholic Voluntary Academy, Marple Bridge

![YoungWriters Est. 1991]

This Is Me

T his is me
H ave long hair
I love animals
S unflower yellow hair

I love dogs, cats, penguins and polar bears
S uperstar swimmer

M e and my family love each other
E njoy baking.

Maria Wall (6)
St Mary's Catholic Voluntary Academy, Marple Bridge

Super Matilda

I am as fast as a cheetah
I am the sneakiest in my family
I have bright yellow hair
I have a big piece of chicken leg
My brother is as slow as a snail
I am as pretty as a devil
I am as happy as can be
I am a big fan of Olivia Rodrigo.

Matilda Stanley (7)
St Mary's Catholic Voluntary Academy, Marple Bridge

This Is Me

I love playing with my scary creeper
I love stroking my puffy dog teddy
My favourite food is hot dogs
I can't stand a day without football
I am inspired by Marcus Rashford
When I eat pizza I love the hot cheese
This is all about me.

Jack Brislane (7)

St Mary's Catholic Voluntary Academy, Marple Bridge

This Is Me

T all and fast
H appy and caring
I am an amazing friend
S upportive

I am always active
S uper swimmer

M y friends are always there for me
E nergetic all the time.

Isabelle Payne (11)
St Mary's Catholic Voluntary Academy, Marple Bridge

Sophie The Excellent

I am an animal lover
I am a superstar eater
I am a polite girl
I am fun to play with
I am like a perfect garden
I am the kindest person ever
My hair is as yellow as a sunflower
My eyes are as blue as the sea
This is me.

Sophie Bradbury (6)
St Mary's Catholic Voluntary Academy, Marple Bridge

This Is Me

T imid to chat
H ate Ed Sheeran
I love everything
S uperstar swimmer

I have ocean-blue eyes
S o artistic

M y favourite animal is a hamster
E yes like an eagle.

Evie Russell (6)

St Mary's Catholic Voluntary Academy, Marple Bridge

Ollie The Amazing

I am a sweet tennis player
I am a super swimmer
I am a bookworm
I love pepperoni pizza
I have eyes as blue as blueberries
I have hair as blonde as a kangaroo
I love dogs
I enjoy playing
I enjoy cuddles
This is me.

Oliver Moores (6)

St Mary's Catholic Voluntary Academy, Marple Bridge

This Is Me

I have a horn but live in the sea
I swim in the great ice, that's just me
I dive down below
And follow the flow
I don't have gills
And I don't have the cold chills
What am I?

Answer: A narwhal.

Anna Webb (10)
St Mary's Catholic Voluntary Academy, Marple Bridge

My Favourite Animal

Nibbling on food
Puts me in a great mood
I am noisy all night
I give people a fright
I will always be there
With fluffy brown hair
I love a treat
When I have a sweet
What am I?

Answer: A gerbil.

Gracie Heaps (10)
St Mary's Catholic Voluntary Academy, Marple Bridge

Dazzling Daisy

I am a dazzling dancer
I am a bookworm
I have a passion for pizza
I have daffodil-yellow hair
I have leaf-green eyes
I love baking
I love dogs
I am as happy as the sun
I think Barbies are the best
This is me.

Daisy Robinson-Bocking (6)
St Mary's Catholic Voluntary Academy, Marple Bridge

This Is Me

J ust can't keep still and an early riser
A lways a good friend
C an't get off my Nintendo Switch
O range is my favourite colour
B MX lover and super fast racer, of course

That is me.

Jacob Russell (8)

St Mary's Catholic Voluntary Academy, Marple Bridge

This Is Me!

Me, me, I am me
When you look at me, happiness is what you see
I like animals and whatnot
Love for the people I care about is what I got
Now that this poem has come to an end
My love for others will extend and extend.

Jemima M

St Mary's Catholic Voluntary Academy, Marple Bridge

This Is Me!

M y favourite animal is a dog

A girl who is fun and amazing

D efinitely not rude or mean

D escribed as a good cook and friend

I love books and biking

E veryone loves Maddie!

Maddie Percy (8)

St Mary's Catholic Voluntary Academy, Marple Bridge

This Is Me

I am a grateful person
I am kind
I care about people
I love football, it is my favourite
I am generous to others
I love my family and friends
I have four brothers, one is very annoying.
This is me.

Isaiah G (9)
St Mary's Catholic Voluntary Academy, Marple Bridge

This Is Me, Free Freddie

T his is me
H ello, my name is Freddie
I am free Freddie
S uper swimmer

I am nice
S uper good

M y name is Freddie
E asy at football.

Freddie Muncaster (6)
St Mary's Catholic Voluntary Academy, Marple Bridge

This Is Me!

I like video games
My favourite is Pokémon

I like eating food
With sugar

I like football
My favourite is midfield

I like reptiles
My favourite is a Komodo dragon.

George Bullock

St Mary's Catholic Voluntary Academy, Marple Bridge

This Is Me!

I am a star swimmer
I am a star
I am a fan of pizza
I have rosy-red cheeks
I enjoy baking
I am a bolting football player
I have brown hair and eyes
I love stroking my cat
This is me.

Charles Whitehead (6)
St Mary's Catholic Voluntary Academy, Marple Bridge

This Is Me

N eed to clean my room tomorrow

O cean is my favourite because I like listening to the sound

A mazing at doing Pokémon Kuro

H appy all of the time because I have friends.

Noah Bullock (8)

St Mary's Catholic Voluntary Academy, Marple Bridge

Little Heart Diana

There are different animals
Cats are my favourite
My second favourite is my family
I can speak four languages
I can do gymnastics
I love Billie Eilish songs
My hobby is painting.

Diana Akhondzadeh (7)
St Mary's Catholic Voluntary Academy, Marple Bridge

This Is Me

I am a very friendly person
I am an extreme football player
I am a lover of school
I love animals, my favourite are dogs
I love to spend time with my friends and family
This is me.

Finnley Chrippes (6)
St Mary's Catholic Voluntary Academy, Marple Bridge

Super Joshua

I am a superstar
I am a lover of cats
Moon Beam is my favourite one
I have hair as brown as a bear
I have eyes as green as emeralds
I love to go on a bike ride
Super Joshua.

Joshua Rose (7)

St Mary's Catholic Voluntary Academy, Marple Bridge

This Is Me

I am good at swimming
I am as kind as a nurse
I wish to see a shooting star one day
I love animals
I am as fast as a lion
I am good at karate
I am good at running.

Jacob Anthony Derwent Chapman (6)
St Mary's Catholic Voluntary Academy, Marple Bridge

This Is Me

A kennings poem

I am a...
Deep sleeper
Early riser
Animal lover
Great footballer
Book reader
Food eater
Holiday lover
Food baker
And finally...
Good friend.

Caleb Rose (10)

St Mary's Catholic Voluntary Academy, Marple Bridge

All About Me

I love dogs
I love cake
I love my family
I love nature
I love football
I love basketball
I love rugby
I love burgers
I love RE
I love everything.

Nico Wilmott-Jones (7)

St Mary's Catholic Voluntary Academy, Marple Bridge

Isaac

I am eight years old
S ometimes I go for a run
A s I cycle, I hear the pounding behind me
A good reader
C limbing is what I like.

Isaac Payne (8)

St Mary's Catholic Voluntary Academy, Marple Bridge

What Am I?

I have a million black spots
I am orange and black
I run at 70mph to catch my prey
I have claws as sharp as a knife
When I run I can't stop!
What am I?

George Oates (10)
St Mary's Catholic Voluntary Academy, Marple Bridge

This Is Me

A kennings poem

I am a...
Good Minecraft gamer
Awesome Lego builder
Great RC racer
Dragon lover
Nerf player
Cat lover
Great outdoors adventurer
This is me.

Quinn Hall (8)

St Mary's Catholic Voluntary Academy, Marple Bridge

What I Love

B ees are my favourite animal
E ager every day to learn
L aughter is the best
L oudness makes me go crazy
A thletics is for me.

Bella Clark (7)

St Mary's Catholic Voluntary Academy, Marple Bridge

This Is Me

I am a superstar dancer
I love my family and friends
I have a passion for pasta
I am a bookworm
I have rosy red hair
I love rabbits
This is me.

Aine Deegan (6)

St Mary's Catholic Voluntary Academy, Marple Bridge

Caleb's Poem

A kennings poem

I am a...
Spider-Man lover
Dessert eater
Fortnite player
TV watcher
Juice drinker
Vegetable hater
Early waker
This is me.

Caleb Smiley (8)

St Mary's Catholic Voluntary Academy, Marple Bridge

About Me

I have blue eyes
My hair is ginger
I can speak four languages
I have freckles
I love turquoise
I am a bit crazy
I like colouring.

Tadhg Curley (7)

St Mary's Catholic Voluntary Academy, Marple Bridge

A Messy Isla

I am amazing at maths
I have a lot of friends
I like to help people
It is better to have friends
My best food is a big fat sausage.

Isla Harrison (7)
St Mary's Catholic Voluntary Academy, Marple Bridge

This Is Me

I am a lightning bolt in football boots
I am a superstar striker
I am a lover of everyone
I am a supporter of everything.

George Muncaster (6)
St Mary's Catholic Voluntary Academy, Marple Bridge

About Me!

J ust love football and golf
A mazing brother
C an play football really well
K ind to everybody.

Jack Challinor (8)

St Mary's Catholic Voluntary Academy, Marple Bridge

This Is Me

I am me
I am fantastic
I have eyes as blue as the ocean
I am hungry for watermelon.

Teddy Carter (6)
St Mary's Catholic Voluntary Academy, Marple Bridge